First American Edition 2017
Kane Miller, A Division of EDC Publishing

Text copyright © 2016 Chris Morphew, Rowan McAuley and David Harding
Illustration and design copyright © 2016 Hardie Grant Egmont
Illustration by Craig Phillips
Book cover design by Latifah Cornelius
First published in Australia by Hardie Grant Egmont 2016

For information contact:
Kane Miller, A Division of EDC Publishing
P.O. Box 470663
Tulsa, OK 74147-0663
www.kanemiller.com
www.edcpub.com
www.usbornebooksandmore.com

Library of Congress Control Number: 2016959846

Printed and bound in the United States of America
1 2 3 4 5 6 7 8 9 10

ISBN: 978-1-61067-658-8

THE TIME SHIFTER

Cerberus Jones

Kane Miller
A DIVISION OF EDC PUBLISHING

CHAPTER ONE

Amelia finished washing her hands at the sink and went back to put up her chair, wiping her hands on her uniform. Around her, it was the usual Friday afternoon chaos. Shani and Sophie F. were still trying to do a bit more on their self-portraits, whereas Charlie had packed up ages ago and already had his bag by his desk, ready to go as soon as the bell rang. The rest of the class were somewhere in between, washing paintbrushes, hanging art smocks and pinning up wet paintings.

Sophie T. weaved between the tables, narrowly avoiding Erik as he flipped his chair upside down and put it on his desk. She was so focused on not spilling the jar of filthy paint water she was carrying that she didn't notice Charlie's bag until she tripped over it.

She let out a little shriek of dismay and went sprawling to the floor, landing flat on the paint palette she had in her other hand. The jar of water slopped all over Dean and sent paintbrushes scattering to the carpet.

Amelia cringed as Sophie T. picked herself up. The whole front of her uniform was now blotched with bright patches of color. Her face was blotchy, too, but that was from the red flush of fury. Sophie T. turned to Charlie, her eyes flashing, and opened her mouth to yell.

"Charlie, you –"

The bell rang loudly. "All right, you all!" called

2

Ms. Slaviero. "Don't forget your notes for next week's field trip."

Charlie grabbed his bag, ignoring Sophie T. completely, and headed for the door. Amelia gave her a quick, sympathetic smile, then followed Charlie out as Ms. Slaviero grumbled cheerfully to Sophie T. and Dean, "Come on, then. Let's get you two cleaned up."

Outside, it was a perfect Forgotten Bay summer afternoon – the kind you wished would last forever. Amelia and Charlie began the familiar walk back up to the hotel.

"The thing about Sophie T.," Charlie said, "is that she's always blaming someone else. She never admits it's her fault. Like, how is it my problem that she's clumsy? Oh wait, that's right – because she *makes* it my problem. And another thing –"

"Charlie ..." Amelia groaned. "Who cares? You

don't have to see her again until Monday. Can't we talk about something else?"

"OK," said Charlie, easily. "I'll tell you what I was thinking about when I was painting: the portrait that used to be in your bedroom. You know, of old what's-her-name."

"Matilda Swervingthorpe."

When the Walkers had arrived at the Gateway Hotel, it was full of the original owner's things from over a hundred years before: massive pieces of wooden furniture, vases, books, artist's easels and loads and loads of paintings. Most of the paintings in the corridors and library were of bowls of fruit and landscapes, but in Amelia's room there was a huge portrait in a heavy gilt frame.

The woman in the portrait had looked very kind, but there was something unbearable about the way her eyes followed Amelia around, especially when she needed to get dressed. So Dad had taken Matilda Swervingthorpe out of her room.

"Matilda Swervingthorpe," Charlie mused. "That's right. I was thinking about how your dad said she disappeared."

Amelia laughed. "Yeah, when he said it, I thought she must have gotten lost in the bush or fallen off the cliff."

"But now it's obvious, isn't it? She must have gone through the gateway. Do you think Tom knows anything about it?"

"Do you think he'd tell us if he did?"

Then, up ahead, Grawk came bounding out of the bushes, his paws covered in dirt. His fur was standing all on end, and a growl rumbled deep in his chest.

"What's wrong with him?" asked Charlie, eyeing the not-quite-a-dog warily.

"I don't know. He's been acting strange lately – like, eating all the time and being super grouchy. He won't even let me scratch behind his ears anymore."

"He sounds like James," grinned Charlie. "Except for the ears bit."

Grawk barked at them and then turned and ran up to the hotel.

Amelia and Charlie knew better than to stand around wondering what to do. Without a word, they hitched up their schoolbags and began to run.

It was a steep hill up the headland, and Amelia had a stitch in her side by the time they reached the gates to the hotel's driveway. Grawk barked again, and Amelia saw that he was standing beside a hole he'd scratched in the long grass off to the left. His tail was stiff and his ears were flat against his head. He growled again.

Feeling spooked, and more than a little nervous of the usually friendly Grawk, Amelia slowly approached the hole. Lying in the dirt only a few inches below the surface was a bright white sphere about the size of a tennis ball. It gave off a low hum and was shining so intensely that Amelia couldn't see its edges. Most amazing of all, it appeared – now that she looked more closely – to not be actually resting on the earth, but hovering a tiny bit above it.

She crouched down to study it, Grawk still growling beside her.

"Wow!" said Charlie, who immediately reached down to grab it.

Amelia slapped his hand away. "Careful!"

"Ow!" Charlie looked at her reproachfully. "Grawk brought us here. He *wants* us to see it."

"He's growling. Do you think he wants you to *touch* it?"

7

Charlie ignored her and quite deliberately
picked up the sphere. Instantly, his hair stood on
end as though charged with static electricity, and
currents of blue light swirled over the surface of
the globe. The look of delight on Charlie's face
suddenly vanished as he jerked his head over one

shoulder and stared behind them. "Who was that?"

Amelia tried to follow his gaze. "What? Where?"

There was nothing to see.

"I thought I saw ..." He frowned. "Here, try it for yourself."

He tossed the sphere to Amelia, who flinched but instinctively caught it. She'd been afraid it would burn her, but it actually felt cool in her hands, and that cool feeling swept up her arms and then through her whole body until even her scalp was tingling. She could tell from Charlie's smirk that her hair must be puffed out like a dandelion too. She felt deeply peaceful, as though her mind were at one with the universe.

And then she saw a flash of movement and had the sense that someone was standing right behind her. She dropped the sphere into the hole and scrambled away from it.

"We shouldn't mess with this," she said,

flattening her hair with both hands. "We should go and get Dad."

Charlie nodded.

"Grawk, will you stay? Guard the hole?"

He sat down obediently, but looked grim about it.

"Good boy," said Amelia, reaching out to pat him. "Thank –"

Grawk turned his head away and closed his eyes, growling steadily the whole time.

"Oh." Amelia pulled back her hand, hurt. She didn't have time to deal with it now, though. Until they figured out what the sphere was, who put it there and why, she had to assume it was a bigger issue than Grawk's attitude problem. "Come on, Charlie."

Leaving their schoolbags with Grawk, they sprinted the last rise of the headland to the hotel and leapt up the main stairs. Forcing themselves to calm down a bit, they paused and then *walked* through the double doors into the lobby.

Just as well. The business was slowly building, and there always seemed to be some new guest just arriving, or wandering around vaguely. More and more humans were coming to stay at the Gateway Hotel, charmed by the thought of a holiday where the natural magnetism of the headland stopped all mobile phones, computers and TVs from working. Amelia's mum and Mary had heard visitors gushing about how refreshing it was to have a "digital detox."

Right now, Mum was talking with a woman at the reception desk, and it was never a good idea to interrupt.

"What's that?" said Charlie, pointing to a large vat by the foot of the stairs to the guest wing.

Amelia shrugged. "Food?"

Some of their alien guests could eat in the dining room alongside the human guests. Wearing the

11

holo-emitters Tom lent them, they were totally indistinguishable from real humans, and lots of aliens were curious to try Earth cuisine. Amelia felt sorry for them that their only experience would be Dad's cooking, but most seemed to enjoy it. Some aliens couldn't digest human food, though, and so, every now and then, special room service had to be arranged. Like their very first guest, Miss Ardman, and her tank of giant centipedes.

"Yes, but what's it doing *there?*" Charlie persisted.

He was right. Any nonhuman food should have either been in the kitchen, or safely delivered to the alien's room. It shouldn't be left out where any actual human might see it and get curious.

Amelia wasn't interested in hotel procedure right now, though. She was too focused on what Mum was saying to the woman at the counter.

"I'm sorry." Mum's voice was very polite, but

absolutely unbudging. "There are no rooms available in that wing of the hotel."

The family wing, Amelia realized. All the guests, even Lady Naomi who'd been there longer than the Walkers, slept in the wing at the top of the right-hand stairs. The rooms at the top of the left-hand stairs were where the Walkers slept. It was totally off-limits to guests.

"But I *so* want a room with a big bay window," the woman said. "And you've told me the bay-window room is already taken on the other side."

Lady Naomi's room, Amelia thought, then stared as she realized what the woman was really saying. *She wants my room!*

She was indignant at the woman's boldness, but not too worried – obviously Mum wouldn't chuck Amelia out of her own bedroom.

"I really must insist," the woman went on. "I don't care how much it costs, you know. Whatever the amount – go on, make up something silly. I'll pay it! *That's* how much my heart is set on it." She put her handbag on the reception desk and opened it, as if Mum had already agreed.

Who does she think she is? Amelia saw a spectacular bracelet sparkling on the woman's wrist as she pulled out her wallet and smiled at Mum.

Charlie tugged at Amelia's elbow, a strange look on his face. "Don't ask why, but I think we should go to your room. Like, *now*."

Amelia didn't want to miss how Mum was going to deal with this pushy guest, but she kind of wanted to go to her room too. More than anything, just to show that woman whose room it really was.

She followed him to the left-hand stairs, but, just as her foot touched the first step, the hotel lobby burned up in a blinding flash of white light streaked through with blue.

CHAPTER TWO

Amelia finished washing her hands at the sink and went back to put up her chair, wiping her hands on her uniform. Around her, it was the usual Friday afternoon chaos. Shani and Sophie F. were still trying to do a bit more on their self-portraits, whereas Charlie had packed up ages ago and already had his bag by his desk, ready to go as soon as the bell rang. He looked up at the clock, his leg jiggling impatiently. The rest of the class bustled around, washing paintbrushes, hanging art smocks, and pinning ...

Amelia froze. She blinked as though she'd just woken from a dream. She gazed over at Charlie and saw that he was looking back at her, frowning in puzzlement.

Sophie T. weaved between the tables, narrowly avoiding Erik as he flipped his chair upside down and put it on his desk. She was so focused on not spilling the jar of filthy paint water she was carrying that Amelia worried she would trip over something. It seemed so obvious what would happen next, so ... *necessary,* that when Sophie T. caught her foot on Charlie's bag and fell, shrieking and sprawling to the floor, Amelia almost felt relieved.

"*Again?*" Charlie said, as Dean stared dumbfounded at the dripping mess on the front of his uniform.

Sophie T. picked herself up from the carpet, ignoring the scattered brushes and the paint smeared all over her as she turned to vent her anger on Charlie.

"*Again,* Charlie? What do you –"

The bell rang loudly.

Yeah … what *did* Charlie mean by "again"? And why did it feel like "again" to Amelia, too?

"All right, you all!" called Ms. Slaviero. "Don't forget your notes for next week's field trip."

Charlie grabbed his bag, ignoring Sophie T. completely, and headed for the door. Amelia gave her a quick, apologetic smile, then followed Charlie as Ms. Slaviero grumbled cheerfully to Sophie T. and Dean.

Outside, it was a perfect Forgotten Bay summer afternoon – the kind you wished would last forever. Amelia and Charlie began the familiar walk back up to the hotel.

"The thing about Sophie T.," said Charlie, "is that she's – you know what? Never mind. I don't have to see her again until Monday, do I? So let's talk about something else ..."

Amelia bit her lip and kept walking. She felt a little weird.

"OK," said Charlie. "I'll tell you what I was thinking about when I was painting –"

"Matilda Swervingthorpe," Amelia said automatically. "You were wondering if she disappeared through the gateway, and if Tom knew anything about it."

Charlie stopped dead and stared at her. "Why are you psychic now?"

Amelia stared back, not sure whether to be frightened or not. "I don't know. Why are *you*?"

"Me?"

"Yeah, you," said Amelia. "How did you know Sophie T. was going to fall?"

"Hey, that's right, I did!" Charlie crowed, then looked around as Grawk came bounding out of the bushes, his paws covered in dirt. His fur was standing all on end, and a growl rumbled deep in his chest.

"And I know this too!" said Charlie. "You say he's been all strange and grouchy, and –"

"And then Grawk barks," Amelia went on, "and then we –"

Grawk barked. They ran.

"What's happening?" Charlie gasped as they sprinted up the steep hill to the headland.

"I don't know. Every time I try to think, all I can see is –"

"A blinding white light?" Charlie suggested.

They ran faster, and as they came to the hotel's gates, they both turned instinctively to the left and headed through the long grass towards Grawk, who was waiting for them beside a shallow hole.

"I feel as though ..." Amelia faltered. "I mean,

I think I already know what's in the hole."

"Yeah?"

"Not really. But as soon as I see it, I'll know that it's exactly ..."

They stepped slowly through the grass until they came to the hole.

"... Exactly what you expected," Charlie finished, as they crouched to look at a bright-white sphere about the size of a tennis ball. It was humming quietly, and shining so intensely that Amelia couldn't see its edges.

Charlie bent down and scooped up the sphere, and Amelia knew this was what Grawk had wanted them to do. Charlie straightened up, and his hair stood on end as though charged with static electricity. Currents of blue light divided and swirled over the surface of the sphere, and Charlie grinned before jerking his head over his shoulder. "Who was that?"

Amelia looked. "Nobody's there."

"Then, here – try it for yourself."

He tossed the sphere to Amelia, who flinched but caught it deftly. She'd been half-afraid it would burn her, but actually it felt cool in her hands, and the cool feeling swept up her arms and then through her whole body until even her scalp was tingling. Without looking at Charlie, she knew her hair must be puffed out like a dandelion too. She felt deeply peaceful, as though all time and space were at rest in one place.

Then she saw a flash of movement and sensed that there were people standing right behind her. She dropped the sphere in the hole and edged away from it.

"We shouldn't mess with this," she said. "We should –"

"Go and tell your dad. Yeah."

"Please stay here, Grawk. Guard the hole."

21

He sat down obediently but looked so grim about it that Amelia didn't try to pat him. They dumped their schoolbags in the grass beside him and sprinted the last rise of the headland to the hotel. They leapt up the main stairs, but forced themselves to calm down a bit before they walked through the double doors to the lobby.

"Oh," said Amelia. "This is different."

Inside, Mum was at the reception desk on the phone, and Dad and Charlie's mum, Mary, were on their hands and knees trying to mop up a strange, syrupy black goop that had spilled all over the floor near the stairs to the guest wing.

"Yeah," said Charlie. "But different from what?"

Amelia frowned. "Good question. We'd better ask —"

But Charlie tugged on her elbow and pulled her towards the other staircase. "Don't ask me why, but I know we have to go to your room – *now*."

Without hesitation, Amelia followed him upstairs and through the family wing to her bedroom.

Through the open door, they could see a woman inside. Amelia had never seen her before, and yet she was totally unsurprised.

The woman was standing in front of the rectangle of wallpaper where the portrait of Matilda Swervingthorpe used to hang. When Dad had removed the portrait, they'd found a small safe set into the wall. It was locked, and the key was long lost, and after a while Amelia had almost stopped noticing it.

But now ... The woman was at work on the little door, probing the lock with a slender tool.

"Hey! You're not allowed in here!" said Charlie.

The woman looked up at them, a lazy smile on her face. She raised her head and Amelia saw a spectacular bracelet on her wrist, sparkling

like diamonds.
The woman
pressed the
bracelet with
her other hand
and the room
was filled with
a blinding flash
of white light
streaked
through
with blue.

CHAPTER THREE

Amelia finished washing her hands at the sink, and rocked back on her heels in amazement. Around her, it was the usual Friday afternoon chaos. Shani and Sophie F. were still trying to do a bit more on their self-portraits. Amelia wiped her hands on her uniform and went straight over to Charlie, who was already packed and ready to go, his bag by his desk.

He jiggled up and down on the spot. "Did you feel it, too?" he whispered as she reached him.

"Yeah, but what was it?"

"Hey, Dean, heads up!" Charlie yelled suddenly as Sophie T. weaved between the tables. She was so focused on not spilling the jar of filthy paint water she was carrying that it was almost inevitable when she tripped over Charlie's bag.

Dean, startled by Charlie's shout, had paused a few feet away, and now stared dumbfounded at Sophie T., who was sprawled across the floor in a paint-smeared heap.

"*Charlie*," she seethed, peeling herself off the carpet. "You –"

The bell rang loudly, and Amelia and Charlie looked at each other, bemused.

"All right, you all!" called Ms. Slaviero.

"Don't forget your notes for next week's field trip!" Charlie chimed in, matching her not only word for word, but beat for beat – the same rhythm and tone exactly.

"Smarty-pants," Ms. Slaviero grumbled

cheerfully as she wandered over to help Sophie T.

Charlie grabbed his bag, and Amelia gave Sophie T. a quick, guilty smile before following him out the door.

Outside, it was a perfect Forgotten Bay summer afternoon – the kind that seemed to last forever.

"All right," said Amelia as they began the familiar walk back up to the hotel. "So all this has happened before, hasn't it?"

"Either that or we're both suddenly wicked psychics."

"Psychic doesn't explain why I feel as though we were at the hotel *a minute ago* when it was *later this afternoon*."

"How much do you remember?" asked Charlie, but before Amelia could answer, they both turned to watch Grawk bound out of the bushes, his paws covered with dirt. His fur was standing all on end, and a growl rumbled deep in his chest.

"Let's go!" said Amelia, and they ran after him as he led the way up the steep hill to the headland.

"There's a woman!" panted Charlie.

"And a light," Amelia said. "Two lights?"

"I can almost feel the memory," said Charlie as they came to the hotel's gates and veered to the left. "But every time I try to see what's there –"

"Everything goes white?"

They strode through the long grass to Grawk, who was waiting for them beside a shallow hole. Without even slowing his pace, Charlie swooped down and lifted the glowing white sphere that Amelia had known would be there. Currents of blue light swirled in multiples over the surface of the sphere and it gave off a high-pitched hum. Charlie's hair stood on end and his eyes filled with recognition as he spun around and looked back the way they had come.

"Oh, yes – I see something. Three, now."

Amelia took the sphere from him and felt a strangely familiar and lovely coolness wash through her whole body. She felt more awake than she ever had in her life – as though she weren't awake only now, but awake to every possible *Now* that could ever be. Like Charlie, she looked behind her. She saw faint figures of people floating in the air – like temporary tattoos that had nearly washed away, leaving only ghostly bits of outline here and there.

Three shapes about her size were walking towards her, one after the other. They were like copies, each doing exactly the same thing, but separated by a second or two. Then she froze as she noticed another set of moving transparencies hovering their way towards Charlie.

She turned to tell Charlie what she'd seen, and then saw a *third* set in front of her, on the opposite side of Grawk's hole. They were just as vague and barely there as the others, except for one vivid detail: a spectacular bracelet.

"That woman!" Amelia dropped the sphere back into the hole. "She's in my bedroom, isn't she?"

Dumping their schoolbags, barely even nodding to Grawk, they sprinted the last rise of the headland to the hotel. Amelia was pink cheeked with indignation at the thought of a stranger going through her things. It was bad enough when she came home from school and Mary had changed the sheets or left a neat pile of folded laundry on top of her chest of drawers. Even that felt embarrassing and invasive, like she was a tiny kid too young to care about privacy – and that was when *Mary* did it. And she *liked* Mary.

She definitely didn't like this pushy, time-bending alien creep.

"Can you remember what she's doing in there?"

Charlie puffed beside her.

"Not yet."

They leapt up the main steps, threw open the double doors and barreled across the lobby, heedless of any human guests.

"Hoi! Slow down!" Dad snapped, looking up from his mopping as they swerved around the oozing black puddle on the floor.

"Plenty of work here for any kid who wants his pocket money," Mary added.

But Amelia and Charlie were already galloping up the left-hand stairs, ignoring Mum's disapproving "*Amelia!*"

"What are we going to do?" Charlie asked as they reached the gallery overlooking the lobby.

For a split second, Amelia hesitated. It was a good question. They knew nothing at all about this woman, really. They didn't, for instance, know if this time business was all part of some hilarious practical joke, or if she was actually dangerous. They didn't know why she wanted to get into Amelia's room, of all places –

Amelia stopped. "The safe."

"What?"

"*That's* what she's doing in my room – she's trying to crack the safe."

This changed things. The Gateway Hotel was full of secrets – strange comings and goings by Leaf Man, a Keeper who could travel through the Nowhere; all the things Gateway Control tried to keep them from knowing, some of which were so important that someone had filled the walls and floors and ceilings with cyborg rats to spy on them; there was even a genuine hidden trapdoor in the library annex, for goodness' sake! Amelia knew there was more going on at the hotel than she could possibly imagine, but she could tell pretty quickly when something wasn't right.

And a time-warping alien cracking hundred-year-old safes in Amelia's bedroom was definitely *not right*.

But she still didn't know what to do about it.

She looked desperately towards Lady Naomi's door – Lady Naomi, who might just be the biggest mystery of all, with her secret research out in the bush. But she was kind and brave and hadn't hesitated to help them out before. She was exactly the person they needed to help confront an alien.

Amelia turned back to Charlie. All these thoughts had flown through her mind in only the briefest of moments, but he was already frustrated by the delay.

"Come on, Amelia! We've got to get in there before she –"

"But what if Lady –"

"No," he interrupted. "No way she's home at

this time of the day."

He was right. Whatever Lady Naomi was researching, she started first thing in the morning and rarely came back until well after dark.

So they were on their own. Unless James ...?

But Charlie was already heading for her room.

Squaring her shoulders, Amelia followed him around the corner into the corridor. And saw that her door was shut.

Charlie strode over to it as though he knew exactly what he was doing and said, loudly, "All right, we know you're in there! You might as well give up and come out now with your hands up!"

It was pretty ridiculous, a kid trying to bluff a grown alien that he was some kind of cop, but Amelia admired his nerve.

He banged on the door, wrenched the handle, then turned to Amelia.

"It's locked."

CHAPTER FOUR

Amelia pulled at the handle uselessly, while Charlie kept banging against the door.

"Let us in!" he yelled, which was obviously a pointless request, but Amelia could barely keep herself from shouting along with him, *It's my room!*

Whatever the woman with the bracelet was doing in there, though, she didn't make a noise.

"The window!" Amelia gasped – if the woman hadn't already escaped out of the big bay window, then at least Amelia and Charlie could glimpse her through it. But that would mean leaving the hotel altogether and going out to the lawn.

"We need someone to guard the door," said Charlie, thinking the same thing.

"James is home." Amelia went two doors down the hall to his room, and found him sprawled on the bed with Tom's charts and his own hand-drawn spreadsheets around him as he tinkered with a box of cogs and gears. A set of Napier's bones was jumbled in his lap. He looked up and regarded his sister coolly.

In fact, *coolly* was the only way to do anything in James's room – the place was practically a fridge. After complaining about being too hot to study, James had taken matters into his own hands: he'd rigged up an ordinary desk fan with a huge battery and supercharged the motor so that the fan's blades spun much faster than was truly safe. Amelia was surprised it didn't rise off the table like a helicopter. It was so powerful it had blown a number of James's smaller gadgets right off the desk, and a stack of Tom's papers – pinned down by a geode the size of a grapefruit – were fluttering so violently, it sounded like a library in flight.

"What?" said James.

"Trouble." Amelia didn't have to say any more. James was already on his feet and pulling on a T-shirt.

"What do you need?"

She could have hugged him. "Someone's in my room – can you guard the door while Charlie and I go around the front?"

Charlie started heading for the stairs the moment he saw them coming. "I heard the window opening," he called over his shoulder. "Hurry!"

Amelia and Charlie sprinted back through the lobby (more cries of protest from the three parents) and out to the grass below Amelia's window, just in time to see the woman, whom Amelia now remembered enough to recognize, perched calmly on the edge of the open bay window, at least twenty feet above the ground. In one hand, she held a small black canister. On the opposite wrist, her spectacular bracelet caught the light and sparkled so brightly that for a moment Amelia was blinded.

She blinked, then saw the woman step from the windowsill into thin air – falling two stories and landing on the lawn as lightly as though she'd skipped down a single step. Amelia was so astonished that she stared, openmouthed, as the woman ran down the hill in the direction of Tom's cottage.

"Quickly!" said Charlie, and Amelia snapped out of it, running with him after the thief.

But they had only run as far as the rose garden before she stopped dead again – not only astonished this time, but horrified too. Grawk had burst out from the long grass and was charging at the escaping woman. His ears were flat against his head, his wide yellow eyes narrowed to slits, and his many sharp white teeth were bared in a vicious snarl. He was so swift and sudden that the woman didn't know he was there until she was already falling with Grawk's teeth in the back of her ankle.

The blood drained from Amelia's face. She'd never seen Grawk like this. He'd always been her funny, brilliant little not-quite-a-dog. Now, though, so fast that the wretched woman barely had time to react, Grawk let go of her ankle, sprang up the length of her body and began biting furiously at her *neck*.

Amelia moaned, aghast.

"He's going to kill her!" Charlie yelped, as he leapt forward to help. He was only three feet away from them when Grawk wrenched his head back, his teeth clamped together. Amelia expected such a violent action to be followed by a spray of blood, but what flew through the air instead was a tiny clockwork cylinder.

He isn't trying to kill her, Amelia sighed. *He is tearing off her holo-emitter!*

Grawk pounced again, this time at the woman's hand, and then bolted off towards the bush, the stolen black canister in his mouth.

Closest to the fallen woman, Charlie was the only one who could see the shape she'd reverted to when the holo-emitter was torn out. He gave a strangled cry and stumbled backward through the long grass as fast as he could.

"Amelia! Charlie!"

Behind her, Amelia could hear the frightened, cross voices of all three parents, coming closer. She didn't turn her head for even a second.

Though she was glad to have the adults coming to the rescue, she knew they were still too far off to be of any real help. Charlie gasped again in fear as the alien calmly rose to its feet.

It was like oil climbing into the sky – impossible, beautiful and *wrong.* Sunlight scattered into tiny rainbows as it bounced off the matte-black skin, and the alien arched its long, elegant neck and rolled its shoulders as thought it had been cramped inside its holo-disguise. A long, sinuous tail flicked in the grass.

Krskn! Amelia knew they were all as good as dead. Or rather, they'd be better off dead than let Krskn get his revenge on them for last time.

Amelia heard a little whimper and realized it was coming from her. The alien turned to them, and Amelia saw its huge jewel-colored eyes were blue, not red, and that its skin wasn't uniformly black. Dappled along its – *her?* – throat and belly

were leopard spots of electric blue.

Not Krskn, Amelia realized. *But one of his kind.*

Now that she looked more closely, differences were obvious. Not just the blue spots – where Krskn had been as wiry and lithe as a trapeze artist, this creature was *thin*. And where Krskn's red eyes had been hypnotically focused and intense, these blue eyes were slightly glazed, as though the mind behind them was somewhere else.

Still behind Amelia and Charlie, but closer now, Mum cried out fiercely, "Don't you touch those kids!"

The alien sighed and clicked her tongue in frustration as she glanced in the direction Grawk had taken the canister. She pressed her spectacular bracelet, and Amelia braced herself for the blinding flash of white light streaked through with blue.

CHAPTER FIVE

Amelia finished washing her hands at the sink, and shuddered with relief. She and Charlie were safe.

But no one at the hotel is, she realized.

"Not again!" came Charlie's voice from across the room, loud and careless in his exasperation.

"Hey, Charlie," said Sophie T., weaving her way between the tables with her jar of filthy paint water and the palette of paint. "When are you going to stop being such a total weirdo and yelling random stuff?"

"Hey, Sophie T.," he snapped back. "When are you going to stop being such an epic fail and chucking paint everywhere?"

Amelia held her breath as Ms. Slaviero raised a puzzled eyebrow, but Sophie T. just gave him a pitying look.

"*Seriously*, Charles? Do I *look* like I'm throwing anything anywhere?"

Then with a great show of condescension, she stepped right over Charlie's bag and as far away from him as she could, sighing heavily.

Charlie couldn't have cared less. Like Amelia, who by now had grabbed her bag, he just wanted to get back to the hotel.

The bell rang loudly.

"Yep!" Charlie said briskly over his shoulder to Ms. Slaviero as he and Amelia headed straight for the door. "Field trip notes for next week – we're on it."

"What do you remember?" said Amelia as soon as they were past the school gates. They were both walking fast.

"Danger," said Charlie. "I know something really bad almost happened. Or is it about to happen? I'm not totally sure ..."

"Same as me." Amelia nodded. "I've got flashes, but it's a bit muddled."

"But we have done this before, right?"

"I think so. And I think we're getting better at it."

They jogged a little faster.

"I remember that woman," said Charlie. "And that bracelet thing – she's controlling all this, right? And ..." he fell silent.

"Something like Krskn?" said Amelia. "Yeah, I remember that too."

"Who could forget?"

"Well, everyone apparently. As far as I can tell,

no one else has a clue that we're stuck in some … loop or whatever."

"Grawk knows," said Charlie, watching as the not-quite-a-dog bounded out from the bushes, his paws covered in dirt.

Amelia looked at Grawk with apprehension. There was something strange going on with him, and, though she couldn't remember why, Amelia now felt slightly scared of him. Not because he'd been moody and sour lately, but because she suddenly realized that no one knew exactly what he was capable of – or what he might become.

"But why us?" she puzzled. "Why do we remember and no one else?"

They thought hard for another few steps, then cried out together, "The sphere!" and pelted as fast as they could up the steep hill to the headland.

Grawk led them to the hotel's gates and over to the left, but by the time he had stopped at the shallow hole in the grass, Amelia knew exactly what to do.

She and Charlie bent together to pick up the glowing white sphere, and in their two cupped hands they saw currents of blue light marbling its surface. It made a shrill whining noise, and their hair stood on end as coolness washed over them. Amelia felt a dizzying rush of knowledge, as though she had stepped out of time itself and could see all eternity laid out like a map in front of her.

Keeping hold of the sphere, she turned to look behind her. Eight figures were walking towards them: two sets of four, walking in single file, one set heading for Amelia, the other for Charlie. The figures were all translucent, so that as Amelia looked at the ones going for Charlie, it was like looking through gauze. But then she saw the ones coming for her, all four lined up, and in overlapping they became substantial enough for her to see clearly.

"It's *me*!" she gasped. "Oh, and that must be you. It's like the trace left behind from the other times we've been here. So –"

She turned to see the Krskn woman. Yes, there she was. Amelia saw her trace selves lighting up the sphere and dropping it, and the sphere disappearing through the grass and into the earth. "Look, Charlie – there she is, starting it all."

"So let's go end it all," he said, dropping the sphere back into its hole.

"How can we? She knows we're on to her, and as long as she has that bracelet, she's always a step ahead of us."

"All right, then, so what do we do?"

"Tom," Amelia said simply, and they both ran.

It was only a short crash through the grove of magnolia trees to reach Tom's cottage, and it felt great to Amelia to finally be doing something different – like they were changing the game, making their own decisions rather than merely reacting to the alien's.

Across the clearing, Amelia thumped on Tom's door, but Charlie just threw it open, and Amelia followed him in.

"What do you want?" Tom growled, not even looking up from his charts. It wasn't the friendliest greeting, but it was actually better than his usual.

"We need your help," said Amelia.

"You'll have to wait, then. There's a dangerous connection about to align."

"How's it dangerous?" said Charlie. "Like, an earthquake-y wormhole, or an unstable one with blowbacks?"

Tom finally sat up straight, pushed the charts away, and swiveled his chair to glare at them. "Neither. The wormhole is solid – one of the most reliable ones we have. The problem is, it connects with MN-5."

Amelia blinked.

Tom looked grimmer still. "MN-5," he said bitterly, "was a major Guild stronghold, back during the –" he caught himself "– trouble."

Trouble? What trouble? Amelia had no idea what Tom was talking about, but by now she knew better than to interrupt him with questions. The trick was to listen and remember now, and try to figure it all out with Charlie later. *If* they could remember it later ...

"By the time Gateway Control got organized, the Guild was a thing of the past. Or so we thought. Now we hear that MN-5 is active again. No one's saying it's Guild, of course. No one's careless enough to say anything like that out loud, but mark my words: anything that comes out of MN-5 is no friend to us."

Amelia gulped. "I think someone like that is already here."

"What do you mean?"

"Someone's messing with time," said Charlie. "This is the first time we've come to you, but we've done everything else like five times."

"You're saying events are repeating?" said Tom, a glimmer of recognition in his single remaining eye.

"Yes," said Charlie.

"And you *remember*?" said Tom.

"*Yes*," said Amelia.

"Then you must have found the recursor."

"The what?" said Charlie.

"The time-control device."

"Mm ... what's it look like?" Charlie asked, shiftily.

"I have no idea," Tom said dourly, brow furrowing over his eye patch. "They're insanely rare, expensive and dangerous. But seeing as you know what's going on, you must have not only seen the recursor, you must have *touched* it."

"We have," Amelia admitted.

Tom snorted and shook his head. "Hopeless. Don't you two listen to anything I say? *Touching* alien technology before you know what it is? You'd be better off running around the bush trying to catch snakes with your bare hands."

"On the other hand," Charlie said in a sarcastic voice, "*thanks, kids, for discovering we're all stuck in a time loop with Krskn's twin.*"

Tom turned white. "What did you say?"

"Last time, Grawk bit the holo-emitter off the bracelet woman and she turned into the same sort of alien as Krskn," said Amelia.

Tom held up both hands. "Whoa, whoa, whoa! Start again: what woman?"

Jittery with impatience, not knowing how long they had before the woman reset time on them again, and not seeing the point in explaining it to Tom if he was only going to forget it all anyway, Amelia hurried through the story as best she could recall it.

"She was in your room?" Tom gasped. "Trying to unlock the safe door?"

He slumped in his chair as Amelia went on, then sat bolt

upright, his face stark with terror. "She got it *open?*"

"She had a black can thing when she jumped out the window." Charlie shrugged. "I don't think she got *that* open, but I suppose she got the safe open to get it."

Tom groaned but gestured for Amelia to go on.

"So then Grawk stole the thing from her and ran away with it, and we all saw that she was like Krskn, only with blue eyes instead, and then she pressed her bracelet and ... that was it."

Tom rubbed his forehead wearily. "Too old for this now ..."

"So what do we do?" said Amelia.

Tom looked up, and Amelia was shocked to see that instead of his normal grumpy expression, he appeared utterly defeated.

"I don't know," he said, shoulders sagging. "I told you, recursor technology is rare and dangerous. Obviously, it's highly illegal, too.

Creating a localized temporal field, like a bubble, and manipulating the fabric of time and space within it – well, it's beyond risky. Each instance of rewinding time inside the bubble wears away at the connection between the bubble and the rest of existence. Rewind time once or twice, you might get away with it – the bubble might just slide back into the flow of the universe when you turn the recursor off. But each time after that, you increase the chance of tearing a hole in existence itself."

"Meaning what?" Amelia asked quietly.

"No one knows. It could be that you tear a new gateway into being, or that you let the Nowhere leak into our world. It could be the start of a black hole, or perhaps the bubble just pops free of the rest of space and time and we spend eternity reliving the same fragment, over and over. There are lots of different theories, but as each of them is equally terrible and unthinkable, no one has ever gone far enough to find out. So. How many times do you think she's used the recursor so far?"

Amelia and Charlie looked at each other.

"We saw ..." She paused to recount in her head, just to be sure. "We saw four copies of ourselves."

Tom closed his eye. "Four times, then. Heaven help us."

"So should we just let her steal that thing?" said Charlie. "Whatever it is, it can't be worth letting her tear up time forever?"

"No!" Tom blurted. "The opposite! Better we all be sucked into a black hole or lost in the Nowhere than to let that canister fall into the Guild's hands!"

"But that won't happen," Amelia soothed him, her own heart pounding at the fear Tom had for this Guild. "The woman must know better than anyone how dangerous it is to keep using the recursor. Surely she won't risk destroying herself just for some robbery."

"You saw her," said Tom. "She's like Krskn – do you think Krskn would care about risk, however bad the odds?"

"Well ..."

"And worse than that," Tom went on, "if she's a time-shifter – I mean, if she's done this before, somewhere else – then she's far more dangerous than Krskn himself."

"Why?" said Charlie.

"Because the time-shifting becomes addictive, they say. That ability to control time, the feeling of power and insight it gives –"

Amelia thought about the tingling rush of awareness and wisdom she had felt touching the recursor, and swallowed hard. Oh yes, a being could easily get addicted to that experience.

"I don't know," Tom went on. "I can only guess what the thrill would be for one of those punks, but from what I hear, time-shifters get so arrogant that they start to think they're invincible. If they go too far with the recursor, they don't get more cautious – it's the opposite! They're more convinced than ever that they have everything under control."

"I thought no one had gone too far before," said Charlie.

"Not in one place, at one time, no," said Tom. "But several years back, a rumor came through Control that they'd managed to catch a time-shifter. He'd become so addicted to the recursor that he kept rewinding time, just once in each moment, but for periods of time so close together the Keepers had notified Control that the Nowhere was being affected."

"So what do we do?" Amelia asked again. "Stop her or let her go?"

"We should break the bracelet!" said Charlie.

"But does she have the canister again this time?" said Tom. "Where is she up to?"

They heard Grawk bark in the distance.

"Last time she got it, she headed here," said Charlie. "So I think we're about to find out."

CHAPTER SIX

Amelia and Charlie were already halfway to Tom's front door, anxious to see what was happening with Grawk and the Krskn woman, when the cottage seemed to sigh.

Instinctively, all three of them stopped and turned to face the gateway room – a bare space visible through the doorway at the far end of Tom's main room. There was nothing in there but a dark shadow in the corner where the wooden floorboards stopped and a stone stairwell led down into the cave system beneath the cottage.

Amelia breathed in and smelled the cold, strange air of another planet seeping from beneath the gateway room's door. The wormhole from MN-5 had aligned.

Tom waved his hand frantically at Amelia and Charlie. "Get back! Get down!" he mouthed, pointing to the little alcove that was his kitchen.

As quietly as they could, Amelia and Charlie slid around the counter and crouched down. Tom walked past them to the front door, opened a narrow panel in the wall next to it that Amelia had never noticed before, and took out a shotgun.

Charlie gasped. "A gun?"

Tom glared at him furiously and made a "zip it!" motion over his own mouth.

Amelia felt sick to her stomach. She bit her lip and tried to breathe steadily so she wouldn't start to panic, but there was something grim and terrible about watching someone you knew pick up a weapon and – what? Were they about to watch Tom *shoot* someone? Or, even worse, about to watch Tom being shot instead?

But she said nothing, just sat crouched next to Tom's pots and pans, listening desperately. There was no further sound from Grawk outside, but that didn't mean much. He could be as silent as an owl when he wanted, and now that Amelia thought about it, he hadn't even made a sound when he'd bitten the Krskn woman last time.

Amelia was assuming that if the Krskn woman had managed to get around Grawk this time, she'd be heading for the cottage – undoubtedly intending to catch the MN-5 connection. Amelia didn't know how long this wormhole would stay in place, but that must be another reason time was so important to the thief: it wasn't enough for her just to steal the canister, she had to get it done within a strict timeframe.

Maybe that was why she rewound time the first couple of times when nothing had really gone wrong with her plan – she'd just been slightly delayed by Mum, or by Amelia and Charlie bothering her in the bedroom. Which meant that either the connection with MN-5 was going to stay open only a very short time, or the people the Krskn woman was dealing with were so dangerous, she didn't dare be late for them.

Either that, thought Amelia, *or she has become so addicted to the recursor that any old excuse will do to rewind time.*

A dreadful possibility occurred to her then: she and Charlie had seen the shadows of their other selves, one for every time they had found the recursor. But what if there had been *other* times, when they hadn't found it? What if, instead of being the fourth time around the loop, it was just the fourth time they knew about? What if they were really up to the twelfth, or the twentieth, or the fiftieth time, and it was already too late to stop her?

What if ... Amelia gulped. *What if this bubble of time has already drifted away from the rest of existence, and we're already trapped here forever?*

The feeling of panic increased. Amelia forced herself to hold her breath and count to ten. No – if they'd drifted out of existence already, how could a gateway connection have just opened up from halfway across the galaxy?

Tom limped softly back to the main room, the shotgun held ready to fire. He looked very familiar with the firearm, as though it were quite comfortable for him to nestle the stock of the gun into his shoulder and walk with his one eye sighting along the barrel. Concentrating hard on her breathing, Amelia couldn't help but wonder what Tom had gotten up to during that *trouble* years ago.

Beside her, Charlie began to shift, and Amelia knew he wouldn't be able to sit still much longer – and yet, apart from the constant ticking of all Tom's clocks, there was total silence in the cottage.

There's no reason to think anyone is coming through from MN-5, Amelia assured herself. *It's just the Krskn woman leaving. Tom's not going to shoot her, he's just being cautious ...*

And then sound exploded through the cottage, shockingly loud and brutal.

Charlie leapt to his feet to look over the kitchen counter, and even as Amelia thought what a silly thing to do that was, she realized she was standing next to him. Tom was standing in the gateway room, pumping the shotgun to reload. The wall above the stairwell was a mess of torn plaster, shrapnel and scorch marks from the gunpowder. *That's* how closely Tom had fired.

But at what? There was no other person in the

room that Amelia could see.

"Tom?" Charlie called.

"Get out!" he barked, pointing the gun down the stairs. "Now!"

But Amelia couldn't move. She was so fascinated and horrified that she could only stand and watch as a silent wave of water lifted itself out of the stairwell. Perfectly transparent, it rippled upward until it was higher than Tom. It was like one of those nightmares where everything happens in slow motion, and it was quite beautiful – though that just made it more terrifying.

Very gently, without any hurry, the water gathered itself into the shape of a human being and reached out for the barrel of Tom's gun.

Tom fired again, blasting through the body of the thing. The alien staggered, shock waves distorting it so badly that Amelia thought it would collapse into a puddle, but in less than a second it had reformed itself and stepped into the gateway room. It snatched the gun out of Tom's hands.

Tom grunted, retreated slightly, and then threw himself at the alien. Amelia thought he was trying to grab the gun back, but Tom went for the water creature's legs in a sort of desperate rugby tackle.

Being completely fluid, the creature simply flowed out of Tom's grip. It dropped formlessly to the floor, washed along about six feet past him, then rose up again in its blank human shape. Tom landed heavily on the floor, his arms in an empty embrace. He was too slow to put out his hands to catch himself, and Amelia heard his knees and forehead hit the wood floor. He let out a moan, but before he could move, the water creature lifted a transparent arm towards Tom.

Tom was much farther from the alien than the length of a human arm, but this watery limb kept stretching out, longer and longer, until it was a liquid crystal tentacle, tapering off to a point like a needle. Tom raised his head and was about to get up when the tip of the tentacle tapped him on the shoulder.

The effect was instant.

Tom slumped to the floor, motionless.

Amelia and Charlie also hit the deck, their legs giving way in shock, so that they were hidden behind the kitchen counter once more.

The door to the cottage flew open, and the Krskn woman – still appearing human – leapt inside. Grawk hadn't gotten her holo-emitter this time. She was less than six feet from Amelia and Charlie, and if she had looked down there would have been no chance of escape for them, but the woman never looked. Amelia couldn't tell whether she was so brimming with confidence from the recursor that she had forgotten to check her surroundings or was just too focused on looking for the water creature. Amelia only knew she was grateful.

"You're late, Trktka," said a bubbling voice that had to be the water creature.

"Late?" Trktka scoffed, walking farther into the cottage and (thankfully) past the kitchen alcove. "Early, late – what do these words mean to me?"

"Do you have the Essence?"

If it meant the black canister, Amelia knew Trktka must have it, seeing as she hadn't triggered the recursor.

Trktka nodded, switching off her holo-emitter and stretching her neck out as her true form reappeared.

"At last!" the water creature burbled. "Well, then, come along. The Guild are –"

But a flash of black had streaked into the cottage, and suddenly there was chaos. Peeking out past the edge of the counter, still on her hands and knees, Amelia saw that Grawk had knocked Trktka down, forcing the canister from her hand, and was now launching himself at the water creature.

Stuffing her fist in her mouth, Amelia expected to see Grawk paralyzed as easily as Tom has been. But Grawk was unstoppable. A kind of wild fury seemed to have come over him, and he charged through the water creature so fast it had no time to evade him. It staggered and Grawk turned and forced his way back through it a second time before it could recover. Tom, Amelia noticed, had not moved during any of this. His eye was open, unblinking.

Grawk was pouncing a third time when Charlie bolted out from the kitchen, heading for the black canister.

But Trktka was getting to her feet, her eyes slitted in anger, her tail lashing.

Charlie was almost at the canister when Trktka

snapped out one hand and threw him hard against the cottage wall, where he collapsed among boxes of clocks.

Amelia thought he'd been knocked unconscious, but to her relief Charlie groaned and looked fearfully up at Trktka. The alien's chest was heaving as she stood over him, and the blue markings along her neck flared violet. Amelia saw what Tom had meant about her being more dangerous than Krskn – not because she was stronger, or smarter, or faster than he was, but because she was on the verge of *losing it*.

Grawk, seeing the problem, leapt between them, standing protectively before Charlie, his fur drenched by the water creature. He narrowed his yellow eyes and growled ferociously.

Amelia knew she had to do something – but what? Tom was down and scarily still, Charlie was hurt and cornered, there were two aliens about to get away with something catastrophic and only one Grawk to stand up to them. Amelia couldn't see any way to save the day. Her only advantage was that neither alien knew she was there – and that only stayed an advantage as long as she did nothing.

Trktka suddenly laughed. It did nothing to make her sound less crazy. "Oh, Frrshalla, what have we become that the Guild has sent us out against pups? We're being paid to fight an old man, a boy and a baby grawk. I feel rather insulted."

Charlie struggled to sit up, pushing the boxes off him. He had a bad cut over one eye, and blood was trickling down the side of his face.

"*That's* not an insult," he said, his voice shaky but the tone as rude as could be. "*This* is an insult –"

But without Grawk to keep splashing it into disarray, the water creature, Frrshalla, had reformed. Charlie, his eyes fixed on Trktka, didn't see the glassy finger worming its way towards him.

He was just pulling himself to his feet to deliver a truly wicked mouthful of insult when the tip of the water tentacle hardened into a tiny point and jabbed him in the neck. It was as though someone had flicked a switch: Charlie dropped bonelessly to the floor.

Amelia flew from the kitchen.

Before even Grawk could react, in a rush of pure, focused rage, she threw herself at Trktka's back and grabbed for that grotesque bracelet. Sure that she was about to tear a hole in the universe itself, and not caring at all, Amelia wrapped her hand around Trktka's whole wrist and squeezed. She was filled with vicious satisfaction as she was blinded by a flash of white light streaked through with blue.

CHAPTER SEVEN

As the water hit her hands, Amelia let out a low sob of grief. She spun on her heels and turned frantically to look for Charlie –

He was there, white-faced by his desk, his hand over his eye. Without warning, he stumbled and gave a groan of agony.

"Charlie?" said Ms. Slaviero, alarmed. "Are you –"

"We've got to go!" Amelia yelled. She was vaguely aware of the whole class gaping at her, but it was totally irrelevant.

Without waiting for the bell to ring, or

bothering to grab her bag, Amelia ran to Charlie and pulled him from the room.

"Amelia!" Ms. Slaviero cried out after them, but Amelia ignored her.

Charlie lagged heavily for a few seconds, and Amelia had to drag him along, but he rallied by the time they reached the school gates. Together they ran with hectic speed up the steep hill to the headland. Grawk joined them halfway, bursting from the bushes as they passed. He gave Charlie an anxious sniff, and then bolted ahead of them to the gate.

This time, when they reached the hole, Amelia's ears rang with the shrill whine of the sphere. She saw it glowing blue, shot through with swirls of white.

"Do we pick it up?" Charlie asked. "I remember everything already."

"No," said Amelia. "We destroy it."

77

"We can't!"

"We have to. You heard what Tom said about using a recursor more than *twice* in one place and time. And as long as Trktka can rewind time, she'll just keep going until she wins."

"But –" Charlie stopped, gulped. "It's just that –"

"What?"

"Well," he said in a rush, "it's just that if you break the recursor and I get killed again, I won't get another chance."

Amelia stared. "You were *dead?* I thought you were just –"

Charlie shrugged, not meeting her eyes. "Look, I don't know, OK?"

"You died ..." Amelia whispered. "And Tom ..."

Charlie drew a shuddering breath, then squared his shoulders and looked hard at Amelia. "But it doesn't matter, does it?"

"Of course it does!"

"No," he said. "It doesn't." He looked at the recursor with loathing. "You're right: if this thing goes around once more, we might as well all be dead. So, whether we break the recursor now or not, the stakes are exactly the same as they always are: *real*."

Amelia dithered. In her head, she knew they had to break the recursor – the logic was clear. But in her heart, she couldn't bear the thought of destroying the only chance to save someone from whatever was about to happen.

"I'm not sure ..."

"I am," said Charlie, and smashed the heel of his school shoe through the recursor where it hovered in its hole.

Amelia braced herself for an explosion of some sort, but the recursor quietly crumpled in on itself with nothing more than a vague crunching sound. When Charlie pulled his foot back, she saw it had disintegrated into a small pile of glittering crystals, as harmless looking as bath salts.

At once the air was still, the recursor's piercing whine silenced.

"Well," said Charlie, very pale and solemn. "That's that."

Amelia patted his shoulder awkwardly.

"Right," he went on. "Last try – let's make it count. And this time, I've got an idea."

"Go on."

"We don't have time," said Charlie. "I mean, now we *really* don't have time. You go straight to Tom's and tell him everything. I'll meet you there."

Amelia nodded, and ran across the lawn to the magnolias, and Charlie headed uphill to the hotel. Grawk cut across the headland, passing the hedge maze, and disappeared in the direction of the bush.

Crashing through the undergrowth and across the clearing, Amelia burst into Tom's cottage and found him sitting back at his desk, poring over his charts.

"What do you want?" he growled, not turning around.

"A time-shifter is coming. She's stealing the canister from the safe in my bedroom, then coming here to meet a water monster from MN-5."

Tom swiveled in his chair and stared at her.

"Quickly!" Amelia urged. "Only don't bother getting your shotgun – it didn't help at all."

That seemed to convince Tom, and he pushed himself out of his chair without arguing. "The recursor –"

"Charlie destroyed it. We've already gone around too many times, so –"

Tom nodded and said something amazing:

"Good work. That was clear thinking."

Amelia was so shocked by the praise, she blurted out, "But we shouldn't have! Tom, last time – I think you got killed!"

Tom stiffened, but then nodded. "Still the right thing to do. You have to make tough calls in battle, and you did. And now, this time, I'll be better prepared. Tell me about the water alien."

"It looked like pure water, but it could take on any shape, and it got you and Charlie by just touching you with one tip of itself. I don't think it's poisonous, though, because Grawk jumped through it over and over."

"A Breel," said Tom.

"It was called Frooshall or something, and the time-shifter is the same as Krskn. She's called Trktka."

Tom's face, if possible, looked even grimmer. "A Breel and a time-shift-addicted Hkryk, and they're after the canister – no question over the Guild's return now. OK ... what's the plan?"

But he wasn't asking Amelia. He picked up the phone on his desk and dialed. "Skye," he snapped to Amelia's mum. "You've got a Guild operative in Amelia's bedroom – no, don't approach her! She's like Krskn, only highly unstable. Is there any way you and Scott can – no, not capture her, but if you can keep her, I don't know ... *contained* or something. Yes. OK. Yes. No, she's here with me. Of course. Good luck."

"So what do we do?" said Amelia as Tom slammed down the phone.

He rubbed his face roughly, his eye closed. "I don't know," he muttered. "A Breel ... extreme temperature change is the only effective defense, freezing or evaporating. If only I had a laser canon ... a flamethrower, even ..." He looked around his cluttered cottage for an idea. "Do I burn this place to the ground ...?"

"Couldn't we just lock the door to the gateway?" Amelia asked. "Stop it getting through the wormhole in the first place?"

Tom shook his head. "The door only closes off access to this stairwell. The gateway itself occupies a huge cavern beneath us – wormholes can be enormous, you know, and even the smaller ones need room to wag around in. They don't just pop open in a fixed spot. And then the cavern itself connects to half a dozen different tunnels through the headland. You've been in one yourself."

It was true. Under the hotel Amelia lived in, there was another, even bigger hotel carved out of the natural caves that riddled the headland. This mirror hotel was for aliens who couldn't stay above ground with the humans, and it could be sealed off at either end with huge metal doors and flooded with seawater, but –

"There's no time, is there?" Amelia groaned.

"No time, and not enough doors to seal off every tunnel. We could protect ourselves –"

"But only by sending the Breel directly to the hotel and endangering everyone else," she finished.

There was a gentle sigh from the gateway room. A cold, strange air wafted through the cottage, and Amelia knew that the wormhole from MN-5 had just aligned.

It was too late. Even with all her foreknowledge, Amelia hadn't been able to change a thing. The only difference was that this time it would be her dying next to Tom, not Charlie. She was glad that Charlie wouldn't have to go through that again, but she wished she'd known to call out good-bye to Mum when Tom was on the phone. She felt numb.

They waited in absolute silence, and Amelia

wondered if the Breel's touch would hurt. It looked quick, at least. She tried to steel herself for the moment – her time was almost up – second by second. She was getting down to her last heartbeats – if the suspense didn't kill her first …

A crazed scream, half-fear and half-triumph, echoed up the stairs. Amelia looked at Tom in confusion, and then, bizarrely, she heard James yell, "Charlie!"

CHAPTER EIGHT

For a moment, Amelia was so disoriented that she thought James and Charlie were coming through the gateway from MN-5. Then she realized that of course they must have gone through the library trapdoor and the tunnels under the hotel. They were coming up to the gateway from the other side.

What are they doing? she thought, as another puff of air came up the stairwell. This one was somewhat smoky, or cloudy – Amelia coughed. No, it was *dusty*. Ugh, she could taste it now in the back of her throat. *Flour.*

She heard Charlie squawk in alarm, the sound booming in the caves, and then a scuffling of feet, and an almighty crash as something heavy and metallic hit the stone walls.

James yelled, "Run!" and seconds later he and Charlie sprinted up the stairs into Tom's room, both of them white with powder.

"It's still coming!" Charlie shouted. "Run!"

"Go!" Tom ordered Amelia as Frrshalla emerged from the stairwell.

But where was the effortless crystal fluid? Where was the weightless rippling? The thing that came into the gateway room was opaque and sluggish, blobbing its way slowly up the last steps. Its whole body was a cloudy snow globe of half-mixed water and clumps of flour.

Unbelievably, somehow, Charlie and her brother had turned the Breel to ... *glue*.

"Go!" Tom bellowed again, and this time

Amelia ran, following Charlie and James out of the cottage.

The three of them crashed through the door into the clearing. Charlie and James started running, but Amelia cried out, "We can't leave Tom alone with it!"

"Tom's got it under control," said James, but then he doubled back and looked through the window to check. To Amelia's surprise, he began to smile. "Actually, yeah – he really has."

She and Charlie joined him at the window and peered in. It wasn't what she expected. Curdled with flour, the Breel was all but helpless, and Tom was whomping it with a cane like it was an old rug. Amelia grinned with satisfaction. Slow and pathetic looking as it was at the moment, the Breel was still deadly, and who knew what it might be capable of if Tom gave it a moment to regroup?

"It's getting slower every time he hits it," she said, watching as the Breel seemed to solidify yet further.

"Ha!" James laughed. "It's the gluten! We got Dad's extra-strong bread flour, and now Tom's kneading it like dough!"

Amelia grinned. "What did you two *do* down there?"

"We got James's fan," said Charlie, happily.

"It was all Charlie's idea," said James. "He got the flour, and we used the fan to drive it towards the gateway."

"It was like a smoke machine!"

"It was brilliant! It filled the whole cave like a cloud, and once the alien started to absorb it and clog up, we chucked handfuls of flour at it." James grinned, and added more soberly, "Then it tried to grab us."

"And I panicked and chucked the fan at it."

"Well, it worked," said Amelia. "Although, actually, you are both idiots, you know. What if you'd got sucked through the gateway to MN-5? Or worse: the Nowhere?"

"I know," said Charlie. "But what if we'd all sat around waiting to get death-tapped instead? Or let the universe get turned inside out by Krskn's crazy cousin? Or –"

"Hang on," James said, still looking through the window. "Tom might be in trouble."

Amelia looked back and blanched. Frrshalla, pounded into a grubby paste by Tom's cane, had rolled into a ball. At first it looked like the sort of defensive thing an echidna or hedgehog would do, but then the ball began to shiver all over.

"That's just crying, probably," said Charlie.

But the shivering got faster and faster until the ball was vibrating violently. Tom backed away nervously, and then the ball reached a climax and

suddenly began to expel
hundreds of white
pellets, shooting
them out in all
directions, fast
as bullets.

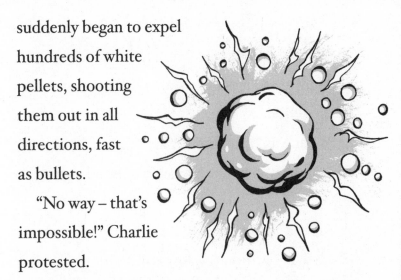

"No way – that's
impossible!" Charlie
protested.

Tom shouted in pain as the stones of hardened
flour pelted him. He stumbled to the door and
almost fell through it to the clearing outside.
Amelia ran to help him, and Charlie slammed the
door closed as the hailstorm inside continued.
There was a muffled rumble as the stones
drummed against the walls and door, and sharp
cracks appeared in the windows as they were
struck. One shattered in a shower of glass shards,
and Tom gasped, "I told you to run!"

"Where to?" said Charlie. "Our plan stopped at the 'turn to glue' stage!"

They heard a distant shout from the direction of the hotel.

"That way," said Tom. "Plan or no plan, we have to stop that canister leaving the hotel, whatever the cost."

Amelia looked at his grizzled face, the black patch over one eye, the hand with a finger missing, that constant limp – were these the costs Tom had already paid defending the gateway?

But this is crazy, she thought. *We're just kids! How can we be expected to –*

"Just run!" Tom barked.

All four of them broke into a sprint, crashing through the undergrowth, smashing heedlessly through the magnolia branches and out to the foot of the steeply sloping lawn. There was a shout – Dad's voice – from the hotel, the sound of breaking glass, and then they were high enough over the rise of the hill to see the hotel and Trktka sailing from the smashed bay window of Amelia's bedroom.

She was in human form and had the black canister in one hand. That wretched bracelet sparkled brilliantly on the other wrist. She landed on the grass as weightlessly as a snowflake, but immediately staggered when – as if out of nowhere – Amelia's mum sprang out from under the cover of the hotel's verandah, spun on one foot and snapped out a lightning-fast side kick that sent the canister spinning from Trktka's hand. Amelia wouldn't have been surprised if the kick had broken Trktka's wrist, but the time-shifter recovered her footing and dealt Mum a ruthless backhand blow.

James growled and ran the last stretch even faster than before. "Don't you hit my mum!" he bellowed, and dived at Trktka just as Dad tackled her from the other side.

It ought to have been a disaster. Krskn would have slid out from between James and Dad and had them both bound and gagged before they knew where he'd gone. Perhaps Trktka was that fast once, but now – her attention on Mum, her concentration fragmented by the time-shifting, and her confidence all smugly set on that bracelet on her wrist – she didn't see the ambush coming.

The two Walker men collided heavily with Trktka, and the three of them crashed in a heap. James immediately scrabbled around to pin Trktka's legs, and Dad practically sat on her back to get her arms. Mum, touching her bruised cheek with the back of one hand, smiled and bent to retrieve the canister.

When Amelia and Charlie reached them, they could hear James and Dad breathing hard as they struggled to secure their grip. Trktka, though, had yet to utter a sound.

"I wonder if she knows about the recursor," Charlie whispered.

Amelia saw Trktka's face contort with effort as she worked to move the hand with the bracelet, and then a gleam of triumph in her eye when Dad grabbed that wrist and squeezed it tightly.

Nothing happened. Trktka blinked in surprise, then thrashed around more violently, forcing Dad to squeeze her wrist still tighter.

Again, nothing happened. Amelia saw panic now in Trktka's face, and she started writhing so ferociously on the ground that her holo-emitter was shaken loose.

"Aargh!" James shouted, almost losing his hold in shock. "She's a Krskn! Dad! You let me tackle a Krskn barehanded?" He floundered for a second as Trktka's tail lashed at him.

"Hold on, James!" Dad urged him. "Don't –"

James wrestled the tail down, but he fumbled, and Trktka used the opportunity to give another huge heave. The arm with the bracelet lifted off the ground.

"Enough of that, you!" Dad puffed. "Just be nice, and lie *still!*" He knocked her arm down and put all his weight into pinning her wrist to the ground.

There could be no doubt in Trktka's mind now: the bracelet was useless. Trktka must have known the recursor was broken. All at once, she went limp and let out a wail of despair. There was no more fight in her now, just grief. Her tail lay flat in the grass.

Amelia almost felt sorry for her. She stopped where she was and just gazed at the miserable alien, her heart full of confused pity, her ears full of Trktka's pathetic sobbing. Even Mum, the canister hugged against her chest with both arms, seemed mesmerized by the scene.

Which is why no one noticed the silent swell of water behind Amelia until the needle-sharp point of a transparent tentacle was an inch from her throat.

"Give me the canister," Frrshalla gurgled, the rest of its body catching up with its arm until Amelia was almost encircled by a standing wave of furious alien. "Surrender the Essence now, or the girl dies."

CHAPTER NINE

Amelia swallowed hard. The skin of her throat tingled in anticipation, expecting at any second to feel that deathly tip of water touch her. If she hiccupped, if she shivered, if she so much as swayed on her feet – it would all be over.

"Quickly!" Frrshalla hissed. "My wormhole won't hang around all day. The canister – now!"

Mum stepped towards Frrshalla slowly and deliberately, her hands out in front of her, holding the canister like any sudden movement would break it. Trktka gave a muffled yelp, but Dad sat more heavily on her back, and she was silenced.

"Mum, no," Amelia whispered. As much as she wanted to be saved, she couldn't let Mum do this.

"Skye! Don't!"

Amelia didn't dare turn her head, but Tom's hoarse shout from far away was unmistakable.

Mum ignored him and kept coming, her eyes fixed on Amelia's. "It's OK, cookie, just hold on," she said calmly, though her face was ablaze.

She stopped three feet in front of Amelia. "All right. Here I am. Now release the girl, and I'll give you the canister."

"No," said Frrshalla. "Give me the canister, and I'll release the girl."

"How do I know I can trust you?" said Mum.

Frrshalla shivered, and the rippling wall of water became a bristling mass of tentacles, all worming weightlessly through the air, each one ending in a lethal point.

"Trust has nothing to do with it," the alien gurgled. "You will do as I say because I am more powerful than you, and you fear me. Now give the canister to me."

Mum nodded meekly and reached out to Frrshalla, her hands trembling as she offered up the canister.

"Mum, please," Amelia murmured. "You can't ..."

Frrshalla gurgled again and took the tentacle from Amelia's neck, using it instead to pluck the canister from Mum. Amelia fell to her knees and scrabbled away as quickly as she could.

"Thank you," Mum said, but as Amelia looked up from the grass, she could see that another three tentacles were hovering only an inch from Mum's face.

"I released the girl," Frrshalla burbled. "I kept that much of the bargain, but tell me: was it worth it? Saving the girl's life for an extra minute or two but knowing that you've lost the canister, that the Guild are victorious and that now I'm going to kill you all anyway?"

"Yep," said Mum.

The Breel shivered all over, the horrible tentacles wavering dangerously close to Mum's defiant face. "What did you say?" it hissed.

"It was unquestionably worth it," Mum said boldly, all her meekness and trembling gone. "The deal making, the careful exchange, this conversation we're having right now – oh, yes, I wouldn't have missed this for the world."

Trktka heaved violently against the grass and undoubtedly would have called out, but any noise she might have made was lost as Dad leaned an elbow on the top of her head and told her, "Shh!"

"Oh," said Frrshalla after a puzzled pause. "Oh, I think I see – this is the famous human banter in the face of certain dea–"

It froze mid sentence and was enveloped by a vast white cloud. Amelia blinked. When the cloud dissipated a couple of seconds later, she saw something extraordinary. Usually, when a person "froze mid sentence" it was just a turn of phrase, but, for some reason, Frrshalla had literally, spontaneously frozen – had actually *turned to ice*.

"No," Mum said dryly. "This is the famous human delay tactic, distracting you long enough that you forget to *look behind you*." She shook her head dismissively. "Amateurs."

Amelia struggled to her feet, completely overwhelmed. Grawk was suddenly beside her, wagging his tail and pushing his warm body against her legs, and then she saw Lady Naomi sheepishly step out from behind the frozen alien, a gas cylinder in one hand.

"What was *that?!*" Charlie whooped in delighted shock.

Lady Naomi shrugged modestly. "Liquid nitrogen."

Mum pulled Amelia into a tight hug, while Amelia asked, "But how did you know?"

"Grawk," said Lady Naomi. "He came bundling up to my research station and kept barking and tugging at my clothes until I did exactly what he wanted."

"It was *Grawk's* idea to get liquid nitrogen?" Charlie asked.

"Well, I had some already, just standing by ... for my equipment, you know ..."

"But hang on," Charlie persisted. "Grawk can *read?* And he knows what liquid nitrogen can do?"

They looked at the obviously not-at-all-a-dog. Grawk sniffed and snapped at a fly, ignoring them all.

"Is the canister safe?" It was Tom, huffing and puffing as he finally crested the hill.

"Well, it's not going anywhere right now," said Mum.

Indeed, the canister was locked solid in Frrshalla's icy tentacle.

"Good," said Tom, smiling as he brought his cane down like a machete. The tentacle shattered, and the canister dropped to the ground in a shower of ice shards.

"Oh, Tom," Mum chided. "Was that really necessary?"

"Yes," said Tom, stooping to pick up the canister. "But this isn't," and he swiped at the alien again.

This time the stick caught Frrshalla diagonally across the center of its body. At first nothing happened. Then there was a deep, glacial creak, and Amelia saw a jagged fault line run through the ice. In a second, that fault had crazed the ice from top to bottom, and with a final shudder, the whole thing collapsed onto the lawn in a pile of icy rubble.

"You killed it?" Amelia gasped.

"If only," said Tom. "No – it'll be fine once it melts."

"Which it's going to do much faster now that you've snow-coned it into pieces," said Lady Naomi, disapproving.

Tom shrugged. "Blast it again with your gas. We've only got to contain it until Control get here."

"Uh, Tom?" Dad grunted. "Don't suppose you could – oof!"

Trktka had started thrashing around again at the word "Control."

"Some rope would be good," James chipped in.

"And cake," said Charlie. "It's been about a week since school finished and we still haven't had afternoon tea. Hey, where's my mum, anyway?"

"Inside with the guests," said Mum. "Poor thing. I have no idea what she's told them is going on out here, but she can't be having fun."

"Yeah, not like us," said Charlie, sarcastically.

"We need some buckets," said Lady Naomi, adding to the list. "This ice is already starting to melt and – *no*, Grawk, *no!* Oh, bad dog! Oh, really!"

Grawk dropped his leg and scratched up some dirt and grass over the shimmering pile of now-yellow ice. Charlie laughed.

"Grawk?" said Amelia, smiling. "Come here, you funny thing." But Grawk only blinked his huge eyes at her. "Grawk?"

He barked sharply, just once, and then bolted away down the hill.

"Well," Lady Naomi corrected herself. "Now we need buckets *and* rubber gloves."

"What about this one?" said James, trying to sound cool and unbothered in front of Lady

Naomi, but actually quite red in the face as he lay clinging to Trktka's legs and tail.

"All right, I'll get the rope," Tom grumbled, setting off down the hill.

"Shall we bring her down to you?" James called after him.

"Not on your life!" Tom snapped. "I don't want her anywhere near the MN-5 connection. Last thing we need is to carry her back to her escape route."

James blushed.

"We still need those buckets!" said Lady Naomi, giving the ice another blast of gas. She looked meaningfully at Amelia and Charlie.

"But what about my cake?" Charlie whined. "Seriously – I will have a meltdown of my own if I don't get something to eat! I mean –"

"Come on," said Amelia, grabbing him by the arm. "The buckets are in the kitchen anyway."

"Oh." Charlie smiled and trotted alongside Amelia to the hotel.

They trudged up the main steps of the hotel, suddenly weary as the adrenaline began to wear off.

"Do you think Control will finally cut us some slack around here?" Amelia asked. Her stomach was rumbling too.

"Just because we stopped an intergalactic robbery, caught two Guild mercenaries and saved the universe itself from being torn in half by illegal time-shifting technology, you mean?" Charlie asked. "Fat chance."

CHAPTER TEN

Ms. Rosby and her team were at the hotel within the hour. As head of Control's department regulating the use of Earth's gateway, she was in charge of any illegal entries and was going to personally escort Frrshalla and Trktka to Control Headquarters.

The other Control agents they'd met had been unpleasant, but Amelia and Charlie were always genuinely happy to see Ms. Rosby.

"Not bad, old man," she grinned, clapping Charlie on the back with one tiny gnarled hand.

The other hand was gripping tightly to her silver-topped cane. "Well done, old girl," she beamed at Amelia.

Amelia smiled back. She knew that she and Charlie must actually seem old to Ms. Rosby who, despite being holo-disguised as an ancient crone, was really only six.

"I couldn't believe it when Tom told me you'd caught two Guild mercenaries. And then when he told me that in fact you had Frrshalla in your jolly freezer in sixteen different ice cream containers packed in among the fish sticks, *and* that you had that ghastly Hkryk, Trktka, tied up like a ballerina's ballet slipper – well, I thought it was an April fool's joke!" Ms. Rosby gripped Amelia's arm tightly as she tottered up the stairs to the hotel. "But then – ah, *then* Tom told me you two had been on the case, and it suddenly all made sense."

"It wasn't just us, you know," said Amelia, wanting to be fair.

"It was *mostly* us," Charlie countered.

"Charlie!"

"Well, I admit we couldn't have done it without Tom, James, both your parents, Lady Naomi, and Gr–"

Amelia coughed loudly. Grawk was one of the illegal, or at least unapproved arrivals on Earth that Ms. Rosby was supposed to stop. If she ever found out about him ...

"Frog in your throat, old girl?" asked Ms. Rosby curiously.

"But, the point is," Charlie went on, "who destroyed the recursor? We did!"

Ms. Rosby was serious at once. "Yes, and we need to have a little chat about that, to be honest."

Charlie was crestfallen. "Did we do something wrong?"

"Heavens, no, man! You did exactly right! But this is the first sign there's been of time-shifting in nearly twenty years. The chaps at HQ thought we'd successfully suppressed the tech. And now we find out that not only was someone out there actively using a fully functional recursor, but it was in service to the *Guild*." She shook her head and paused, just inside the lobby, to catch her breath. "So we really need to know anything and everything you can tell us about the recursor you saw. It's great that we have the remote setting device –"

"Huh?" said Charlie.

"The bracelet," said Amelia.

"Yes, that's a real help, and there's a lot of data we can glean from it, but any details you can add will help HQ determine exactly which model of recursor Trktka was using. If we can trace where she got it, or who helped her get it …"

Dad and Tom came out of the lounge, and

Dad's face lightened when he saw Ms. Rosby.

"Metti!" he grinned, hurrying over. "How's tricks at the office?"

"Same as ever," she said wryly. "I'm sure you can guess: Arxish banging on about needing to intensify Control security at this gateway, those little creeps Snavely and Tavnik agreeing with every word, and me and Stern bored out of our gourds having to go over this ground *again*."

"They still want to shift us out and let them take over the hotel?" Dad said, his smile fading.

Ms. Rosby snorted. "Let them try! I may have wondered aloud how long Frrshalla and Trktka have been on the run. Could it really be *twelve* times they've evaded arrest by our people? No? Thirteen, then, was it? And then I asked how successful our investigations into Guild activities had been – had we, for instance, been able to get any firm evidence that the Guild were organizing a resurgence? No?" She smirked at Tom. "It's quite marvelous to be able to ask these questions and have everyone remember that I'm only six years old. I only started working at Control when I was two, and absolutely none of this nonsense happened when I was in charge, I assure you!

"Anyway, when everyone got remarkably quiet, I simply mentioned – just in passing, understand – that it was the humans who had saved the day."

"Thank you, Metti," said Dad.

Tom nodded fervently.

"Don't thank me," said Ms. Rosby. "I'm thanking *you*. But back to all the hoo-ha here: do you know yet what the Guild were doing?"

Dad and Charlie opened their mouths at the same moment to speak, but Tom said quickly, "No! Not a clue. Nothing's been damaged, as far as we can tell. Nothing's missing ..." He finished lamely with a shrug.

"Really?" Ms. Rosby pursed her lips. "How odd."

She looked sharply at Dad, but he followed Tom's lead and just shrugged.

"Right ..." said Ms. Rosby. "Well, then ..."

"There is one matter I'd like to raise with you," Dad said brightly, taking Ms. Rosby's arm from Amelia and leading her to the kitchen to see the prisoners. "It's ... it's about money, actually. A number of our regular guests were very upset by the, uh, kerfuffle, and Mary offered to cancel all their payments for staying here, and so ..."

"Oh, don't fret over *that*," Ms. Rosby laughed as they reached the kitchen door. Dad grimaced back over his shoulder at Tom.

After a long interview with Ms. Rosby, where Amelia and Charlie were separately questioned three times about the recursor, each answer checked and rechecked until she was quite sure they could remember nothing more, the kids finally got to rest. More importantly, after endless rib-cracking hugs and kisses from Mary, Charlie finally got his cake.

He and Amelia sat down on the foot of the stairs in the lobby, concerned with nothing more than blissfully working their way through vast slabs of banana cake.

"Do you hear that?" said Charlie, after a while.

"What?"

"I thought I heard 'Greensleeves' playing ..."

Amelia listened. She heard it, too.

Curiously, they got to their feet and opened the entrance doors of the hotel. And there was Mr. Snavely – Control's infamous "health inspector" – his pinched little face even more disgusted than usual as he drove up in a cheery pink-and-white ice cream truck.

Actually, it was far simpler than that. Ms.
Rosby had arranged an extremely nice exchange
for the Walkers: Mr. Snavely would empty the
truck's supply of ice cream, sorbet, gelato and
frozen yogurt into the hotel's freezer, and in
return the Control agents would transfer the
sixteen containers of frozen Frrshalla to the
truck.

Trktka was another matter, though.

First Mary had to coax all the guests into the
library, promising them a special historical reel-

to-reel film of Forgotten Bay – "and chocolate!" – as an excuse to keep them all inside with the curtains drawn. Once the library doors were closed, two broad-shouldered Control agents bundled Trktka out under a blanket while she struggled and gnashed at them.

"Thanks for coming, lovely to meet you!" Charlie called as the group crossed the lobby.

Amelia elbowed him in the side.

"What?"

She smiled and shook her head at him. "Does nothing bother you?"

"What do you mean?"

"I don't know." Amelia shrugged, heading for the stairs up to her room. "I just ... After all that, I don't know how you can feel like provoking her."

"Well, she deserves it!" said Charlie, following. "As if a bit of provoking comes anywhere near to what she did to us!"

"No, that's not what I meant. It's more ...
I was really scared it was the end for us today.
You one time, me another, maybe all of us, if we
hadn't broken the recursor ... I'm just surprised
that doesn't upset you more."

Charlie stared at her for a moment, then
dropped his head. "It does."

Amelia heaved a deep breath, and waited.

Charlie shrugged. "I don't know ... maybe
Tom's gotten to me at last, but you know the bit
that I keep going over in my mind? What would
have happened if James and I had fallen into the
Nowhere. It was so rushed at the time, we didn't
stop to think about it, but now ..."

At last he looked up at her. "Do you think we
would have really been lost forever?"

"I don't know," said Amelia. "But I'm glad we
don't have to find out."

They were both very quiet for a while.

They heard Dad come out of the kitchen downstairs with Ms. Rosby, walking her to her car. Amelia crept out across the gallery overlooking the lobby and peered over the railing at the hotel's main doors. She heard Dad and Ms. Rosby farewelling each other, and Ms. Rosby's last "Bravo!" as she drove off down the gravel driveway. Dad plodded back into the hotel and closed the door behind him with a sigh.

Amelia was about to call down to him when Tom limped out from the lounge. "Have they gone?"

"Yes," said Dad. "They've gone. Perhaps now you might tell me why we lied to one of the top three Control agents on Earth? Not only that, but one of the only *two* agents in the whole organization that is on *our side*. Why didn't we trust her with the truth?"

"Because some truths were never meant to be told," said Tom. "And that canister was never meant to be found. Even more than the recursor, what's in it has the power to overturn the universe as we know it."

Dad blinked and his anger fell away from him. "So what is in it?"

Tom looked away. "I don't know."

"You. Don't. Know."

Tom huffed. "Look, it was hidden in that safe years ago – not just before Control was assembled, but years before the war."

Amelia's stomach flipped over. *The war?* What war? Is that what Tom had been referring to as the *trouble?* Had they been fighting against these Guild people?

"Hidden by whom?" said Dad.

"I don't know that either."

"Oh, come on, Tom!"

Tom glowered. "I don't know, I said! Your guess is as good as mine. Swervingthorpe? Who knows? But that safe is late nineteenth century, and the canister has been in there, as far as I know, since then."

"But –" Dad said.

"Look," Tom talked over him. "The Keeper – the one the kids call Leaf Man – told me the safe's contents were to be kept secret. I've spoken to him today. Just before Rosby arrived, he came through the gateway and I thought he was going to tell me that the recursor had set off some crisis in the Nowhere, and now the gateway was going to collapse or something. But no. He didn't even *mention* the Nowhere until I had promised him the canister was safe."

Amelia saw Dad's face phase through about a dozen different expressions as Tom spoke, and she knew his mind was already racing, trying to imagine the math that would explain the recursor. The physics of the Nowhere! You could see how excited he was, how many questions he had for Leaf Man, how curious he was to know *exactly* how the Nowhere had reacted to the repeated time-shifting ...

But Amelia could also see the sheer frustration in Tom's face, that Dad was totally missing the point.

"Scott! Listen to me – what's in the canister, why it's here, who put it there: none of that is our problem right now."

"It's not?" Dad blinked. "Then what is?"

"The Guild!"

That sobered Dad instantly. All the beautiful possibilities of pure science fell away from him, and he came back to the bleak facts. "The Guild..." he said. "Control never mentioned ..."

"No, well, they wouldn't have," Tom said.

"You heard Rosby – they've all been in denial, pretending nothing that bad could happen twice in one universe."

"But now?"

"Now we know that the Guild are back. We know they want that canister so badly they're prepared to break time to get it. And we know they never give up. We stopped them this time, but they'll keep on sending people – thieves, mercenaries, soldiers, *assassins* – until they get it. Which means we have to deal with the canister *first*. And quickly."

Amelia and Charlie gaped at each other, Amelia imagining an infinite line of Hkryk and Breel lining up at the gateway, waiting their turn to attack the hotel. They'd been unbelievably lucky this time – Tom and Charlie had actually cheated death – but how long could their luck hold for?

Amelia hugged herself, mouth suddenly very dry. She and Charlie were hardly breathing – both of them too shocked to say a word, too frightened to move and too anxious to hear what Tom might say next.

Dad let out a ragged sigh, his shoulders sagging. He muttered, "It's happening too fast ... I thought Control said ..."

Tom snorted in contempt.

Dad gazed at him, white-faced. "I never would have brought the kids here, if I'd known."

Tom looked away, and Amelia felt a guilty twinge. From the very start, Tom had been weirdly angry about her and Charlie and James being around. She'd thought he was one of those horrible, bitter old men who hate kids for no reason. But he'd been telling them all along, hadn't he? If only they'd bothered to listen, they'd have heard his warnings loud and clear: *the gateway is dangerous.*

Dad shook his head, then said briskly, "Right. So, what do we do with the canister now? Will you take it?"

"No!" Tom was shocked. "It can't be anywhere near the gateway!"

"No, no, of course not ... but then, where? Will the Keeper take it?"

"I doubt it. He used to come and check on the safe once in a while, but even through the thick, lead-lined door, whatever's in the canister made him sick for hours afterward."

Dad got that faraway look on his face again as he thought over what that might hint about the canister's contents, and then Amelia saw the hotel's main doors open. Lady Naomi slipped inside. Tom turned to see her, and his expression softened.

"Oh, Lady Naomi – just the person I wanted

to see."

She smiled wryly. "Really? Sounds as though you've got a job for me, Tom."

"I do." He put his hand inside his coat and pulled out the black canister. "I need you to hide this."

"Where?"

"That's the point – I don't want to know. I don't want *anyone* to know where you put it."

Lady Naomi nodded and held out her hand for the canister. She looked at Tom solemnly, her face calm and perfectly detached – a strange look of trust and obedience mixed with understanding that the less she knew about what she was doing, the better for everyone. The *safer.*

As Lady Naomi wrapped her long fingers around the canister, though, that calm seemed to flee from her. Her eyes widened, her mouth dropped open in a gasp, and if Lady Naomi had been a cat, Amelia was sure her tail would have been sticking out straight like a bottlebrush.

"Lady –" Tom stepped towards her to take the canister back, but Lady Naomi pulled herself together and tucked the canister under her arm with a short, shaky laugh.

"I'm OK – really! I'll –" She smiled tightly at Tom. "I'll take care of this, I promise."

And without another word, she walked out of the hotel and into the night.

Amelia and Charlie gazed at each other. *What was that?*

Amelia's mum, Grawk, Tom, Trktka, Frrshalla – none of them had reacted in any way to the canister. But Leaf Man did. And now Lady Naomi ...

Dad was right: everything was moving way too fast. Secrets were unraveling all around them, and each secret was bigger than the last.

A *war* had come to Forgotten Bay once. And now Amelia had seen with her own eyes the canister that might very well start a new one.

THE GATEWAY

SEVEN GREAT ADVENTURES

Cerberus Jones

Cerberus Jones is the three-headed writing team made up of Chris Morphew, Rowan McAuley and David Harding.

Chris Morphew is *The Gateway's* story architect. Chris's experience writing adventures for *Zac Power* and heart-stopping twists for *The Phoenix Files* makes him the perfect man for the job!

Rowan McAuley is the team's chief writer. Before joining Cerberus Jones, Rowan wrote some of the most memorable stories and characters in the best-selling *Go Girl!* series.

David Harding's job is editing and continuity. He is also the man behind *Robert Irwin's Dinosaur Hunter* series, as well as several *RSPCA Animal Tales* titles.